W9-ANN-931

The Boxcar Children Mysteries

THE
VANISHING PASSENGER

created by
GERTRUDE CHANDLER WARNER

Illustrated by Robert Papp

ALBERT WHITMAN & Company
Morton Grove, IL

The Vanishing Passenger
created by Gertrude Chandler Warner;
illustrated by Robert Papp

ISBN10: 0-8075-1066-1 (hardcover)
ISBN 13: 978-0-8075-1066-7 (hardcover)
ISBN 10: 0-8075-1067-X (paperback)
ISBN 13: 978-0-8075-1067-4 (paperback)

Cover art by Robert Papp.

For more information about Albert Whitman & Company,
visit our web site at www.albertwhitman.com.

Contents

THE
VANISHING PASSENGER

CHAPTER 1

Not Everyone Is a Finch Fan

Six-year-old Benny Alden lay on the floor of the Greenfield Public Library. He was coloring a huge poster.

"How's it coming, Benny?" asked Violet, his ten-year-old sister. She was holding a poster of her own, which she'd just finished. She gently waved it so the ink would dry.

"Okay," Benny replied. "What do you think?"

He leaned back so Violet could have a look. The words were big and bold, printed clearly in black on the heavy white paper:

TOMORROW NIGHT AT 7:00

COME AND MEET

GILBERT FINCH

AUTHOR OF

"THE YOUNG ADVENTURERS"

SERIES FOR CHILDREN

AT THE GREENFIELD LIBRARY

Benny's sister, Jessie, who was twelve, had actually written the words. Benny was still learning to read and write. But he did add little drawings of Mr. Finch's books.

The Aldens loved Gilbert Finch's books. Each one was set in some faraway place, and the main characters were always children who found themselves in exciting situations.

"It looks great, Benny," Violet said. "I like the little books you drew around the outside. I'll bet Mr. Finch will like it, too."

"I still can't believe he's coming here," said Jessie. She was coloring another poster. "He has so many fans, and yet he's coming to *our* library."

"And all we had to do was ask him," added Henry. At fourteen, he was the oldest of the children. "Violet's idea to simply write him a letter was great."

Violet smiled. "The worst he could do was say 'no.'"

But Finch hadn't said no—he'd written back to the Aldens right away and said he'd be delighted to visit their library. His latest book, *The Lost Chamber of Gold*, was an exciting story set in the jungles of Brazil. Mr. Finch had been visiting other libraries and bookstores all over the country.

"A lot of people will be here to see him tomorrow night," Jessie pointed out. "Ms. Connally said as many as a hundred."

"Maybe even more," said Ms. Connally, who walked into the room at that moment. She was the head librarian and knew the Aldens well. "I just got off the phone with Ms. Pollak, over at the elementary school. She's asking everyone in her class to come."

"Wow!" Benny said.

Ms. Connally walked around to see everyone's posters. "They look very nice," she said. "Where will you put them?"

"All over," said Violet. "Anywhere they'll be seen by a lot of people. The supermarket, the bank . . . "

"The school," Jessie added.

"The gas station," Henry continued.

"And the train station," Benny said. "Don't forget that!"

The Alden children were very familiar with trains. After their parents died, they learned that their grandfather was coming to get them. They heard he was mean, so they tried to hide from him. They picked an abandoned boxcar as their hiding place. When Grandfather finally found them, they soon realized he wasn't mean at all. The children went back to Greenfield with him. Then Grandfather arranged to have their boxcar brought along, too! It was set up in the backyard, where they could play in it anytime they wished.

When Benny mentioned the station, it reminded Jessie of something very important. She checked her watch and said, "We'd better get over there soon. Mr. Finch will be arriving in less than an hour."

"Oh, that's right," Violet added. "He called here earlier to let us know he was getting on the train."

Mr. Finch had agreed to come to Greenfield the day before his appearance so he could have dinner with the Alden children and their grandfather. He'd also said something about wanting to see a friend, but he didn't say who it was.

"Good luck!" Ms. Connally said as she left the room.

The Aldens finished the posters and bundled them together in a neat pile. They would hang them around town as they walked to the station.

As they headed for the door, they noticed someone standing by a display of Gilbert Finch's books. He was an older man, with unruly hair. He wore a pair of small, round glasses, and his shirt wasn't tucked in.

The children had arranged the book display the night before, and they were very proud of it.

This strange man, however, didn't seem

very impressed. Instead, he was moving the books around so that they were harder to see. He turned them so only the backs were showing! And then he took some other books off the shelf and put them up in front of Finch's books. While he was doing this, he kept peering around the corner of the nearest bookshelf. It seemed as though he was worried about Ms. Connally catching him!

When the man was done ruining the display, he walked away quietly.

"What was that all about?" Henry said.

"I don't know," Jessie replied, "but it was pretty odd."

"We should go fix it," Violet suggested.

"Yeah!" Benny agreed in a huff.

They walked over and put everything right again. When they were finished, Jessie said, "We should tell Ms. Connally when we get back."

"But for now," Henry said, "let's get over to the train station. We don't want to be late."

As they reached the front door, they saw the strange man again. He was at the front desk, speaking with Ms. Connally. The children couldn't help overhearing their conversation.

"Why can't I speak at the library, too?" he grumbled. "My books are just as good!"

"I know they are, Mr. Van Buren," Ms. Connally said in a calm, low voice. The children got the impression she was hoping the man would lower his voice.

"You're having Gilbert Finch come all the way down from Clairmont. That's more than two hundred miles from here. I live less than an hour away! I could get as many people in here as *he* could," the man went on. He was also making sharp gestures with his hands, as if his loud voice wasn't enough. "All I ever hear about is Gilbert Finch this, and Gilbert Finch that." He tapped himself on the chest. "What about Daniel Van Buren?"

Ms. Connally took a deep breath. "Mr. Van Buren," she began, "we have an opening in our schedule next month, the night of Sunday, the twenty-third of—"

"What good will that do?" he snapped.

"I'll be busy then! I'm here, now, in town on business. It wouldn't be too much to squeeze me in tomorrow night, would it?"

"I'm sorry, I can't," she replied.

"Ah, forget it," he said with a wave of his hand, and turned away. He stalked past the Aldens without noticing them and pushed his way out the front door.

CHAPTER 2

Vanished!

"That man at the library had to be the rudest person I ever saw," Jessie said as they taped the last poster to a pole at the Greenfield train station.

"He certainly was," Henry agreed.

Jessie checked her watch again. "Anyway, Mr. Finch's train should be arriving any minute. Are we ready?"

"I'm ready!" Benny replied.

"Me, too," said Henry.

"So am I," added Violet. "Except that . . . I'm a little nervous." She laughed.

Jessie said, "I hope the train isn't late. I wouldn't want—"

At that moment, far in the distance, came the faint blast of a horn.

"It won't be late," Henry said.

They leaned forward to get a good look as it came around the bend. Jessie straightened up and brushed off her clothes. "Okay, everyone get ready . . . "

After the train came to a complete stop, the doors slid back, and the conductors stepped off. They wore handsome blue uniforms with gold buttons down the front. Then, the passengers began coming out. There were a lot of them. Some were people the Aldens recognized as Greenfield residents. Others were strangers.

The Aldens didn't know which car Finch was in, so they watched all the doors. Violet noticed a family with a little girl and a little boy get off the train. She could see that the two children were crying. The little boy was rubbing both eyes and pouting. The little girl, with tears streaming down her face, was holding a long leather leash. And their father was carrying what appeared to be a large box with a red blanket over it.

"Hey, look over there," Violet said to Henry.

"Do you see Mr. Finch?" Henry replied.

"No, those two small children. They're crying."

A conductor came over and spoke with the family. He was a friendly looking man, with blazing red hair sticking out from under his conductor's cap. He first talked to the parents, who looked worried. Then he crouched down and tried to cheer up the children. He got two lollipops from inside his jacket. The children took them, but they didn't stop crying.

"I wonder what's wrong," Benny wondered.

"I don't know," Violet said. "I can't hear with so many other people around. There's too much noise."

The conductor stood up again and patted the little boy on the back. The father stroked his daughter's hair and said something to her. Then the conductor led them away.

"How sad," Jessie said.

"Yeah," Henry agreed. "I hope they're okay. But has anyone seen Mr. Finch yet?" He tried to see over the crowd, but he wasn't quite tall enough.

"No," Jessie said, looking around carefully. "No sign of him."

The children moved closer to the train so they could get a better view of all the doors. A moment passed, then another. The crowd started to thin out. Passengers found their friends and families and began leaving the station. Suitcases were wheeled off, and the noise died down. Then the children were alone.

Everyone had now gotten off the train— and Gilbert Finch was nowhere in sight.

* * * *

Jessie said, "Are you sure you didn't see him?"

"I didn't," replied Henry. "And I'm certain I checked everyone."

"Me, too," said Violet.

"Maybe he didn't realize this was his stop and forgot to get off," Benny suggested.

"No," Jessie said, "Greenfield is the last stop for this train until tomorrow, when it goes back up north. There are no more stops. So even if he forgot, he'd still have to get off here."

Henry took a piece of paper from his pocket and unfolded it. He'd written down all the information about Finch's arrival.

"Let's see . . . ten-thirty in the morning, arriving on Saturday, on train number sixteen." They checked up and down the cars. Sure enough, right on the side of the engine, "16" was painted in big white numerals. "This is the right one," said Henry.

"Then where is he?" Violet wondered.

They spotted the red-haired conductor walking down the platform counting a stack of tickets.

"He might know," Henry said, and they jogged over to him. "Excuse me, sir?"

As the man turned, the children noticed for the first time that his uniform was all wet.

"Wow!" Benny said, unable to help it.

The conductor smiled. "Oh, that. There was a storm up north. I only stepped off for a moment, and I got soaked."

"Must've been bad," Violet said.

"It was. One of the worst I've seen this year. Anyway, what can I do for you kids?"

Henry took a copy of one of Finch's books from his back pocket. It was the one he told Mr. Finch he would hold in the air when Finch got off the train so he would be able to find the Aldens quickly.

"Did you notice anyone during the trip who looked like this?" He turned the book around to show the back cover. There was a small photo of Finch, smiling. He was a handsome older man, with wavy brown hair and lively eyes that had a hint of mischief in them.

"He was supposed to meet us here this morning," Jessie told him.

"He's visiting our library," Violet said.

"And his books are really good!" Benny added helpfully.

The conductor laughed. "I have a boy

your age at home, so I'll have to remember that." He took the book from Henry and studied the photo.

"No, I'm afraid not. There was no one in my car who looked like this. You should speak to the other conductors." He pointed towards the station.

"Great, thanks," Henry told him. "Come on everyone."

The Aldens went into the tiny station house, which was very old and beautiful. It had a dry, dusty smell, like an antique store. The children always enjoyed coming down here.

They found the other two conductors sitting together. They were filling out paperwork. Their uniforms were also soaked by the rain.

"That was some storm," one of them said. "I couldn't see anything out the window."

"If my dog heard all that thunder and lightning, he would've hidden under the seats and stayed there, shaking," said the other man. Benny remembered how much their dog, Watch, hated storms, too.

"Excuse me," Jessie said. She explained about Finch. When Henry handed them the book, they all took a long look at the picture.

"Sounds like an interesting story," said one of the conductors. He studied the photo carefully, then shook his head. "I'm sorry, but I don't recall anyone who looked like that."

"Me, neither," said the other conductor.

"Okay," Jessie said. "Thanks, anyway."

They stepped back outside, closing the station door behind them.

"But he got on the train," Jessie said. "Remember, when he called the library earlier this morning?"

"That's right," Henry told them, nodding. "He called from the station and told us he was getting on right then. He wanted to let us know that the train was on time so we could be here to meet him."

"So what happened to him?" Benny wondered.

Henry took a deep breath and let it out again. "Well," he said with his hands on his hips, "that's what we have to find out."

"We should start by searching the train," Violet suggested. "Remember what Mr. Finch wrote in *The Crown Jewels of London* when that professor disappeared? The first thing the little boy and girl did was go to the place where the professor was last seen, which was his office at the university."

"That's right, Violet," Henry said. "Good idea. Let's go have a look at the train."

CHAPTER 3

The Fourth Car

The train had been switched off the main track into a rail yard. There were dozens of other trains there, too.

"It looks like a train parking lot!" Violet said.

"Which is the one we want?" Benny wondered. "There are so many!"

"Number sixteen," Henry reminded them, and soon they found it.

A heavyset man with a bucket and a mop was washing the outside of one of the passenger cars. "Hi there," he said. "You didn't get off at the wrong stop, did you?"

Henry said, "No, we live here in Greenfield. We were just wondering if we could take a quick look through this train."

The man put down his mop and leaned against it. "Did you lose something?" He took a handkerchief from the back pocket of his overalls and patted his sweaty face.

"Yes," Benny said. "A whole person!"

Henry explained the situation. When he was finished, he said, "So we'd like to search the train for clues, and we thought we should ask if it was okay first."

"Well, it's fine with me, I guess," the man said. "I'm just about to clean it out."

"We could help," Violet suggested.

"Since we have to go through it, anyway," Jessie added.

"Sure, that's fine with me. My name's Pete, by the way." He shook hands with all the Aldens, who introduced themselves in turn. "Sure, I'll take any help I can get! Here." He leaned down and grabbed four plastic garbage bags. "One bag for each of you. Have fun."

"Thanks, Pete," Henry said.

The children stepped onto the first of the four passenger cars. The deserted train was a bit eerie inside, even with the sunlight slanting in. Through the door at the other end they could see clear through to the next car, and then the one after that.

"Kind of creepy," Violet commented.

"Yeah," Henry agreed. "You never imagine a train being empty. Anyway, let's get on with our search. Jessie and I will look high, you and Benny look low. We'll go one seat at a time."

The Aldens went slowly and carefully. In the first two cars, they found abandoned newspapers, soda cans, pens, and candy wrappers. It wasn't until they reached the back of the third car that they came across something that might be considered a clue—a copy of *The Secret of the Pyramids*. It was Gilbert Finch's fifth book, set in the ancient ruins of Egypt.

"Wow, look at this!" Benny cried out when he spotted it hidden underneath the very last seat. He handed it to Jessie, who examined it.

"Would he actually read a copy of his own book?" she wondered.

"Maybe he was planning to talk about it at the library," Violet suggested.

Jessie pulled the cover back and saw something scrawled at the top of the very first page: *Property of Mrs. Alice Blake.*

"Alice Blake?" Henry said. "Why does that name sound familiar?"

"She lives two blocks from us," Violet replied. "Remember? She's that nice woman who always gives out great candy on Halloween."

"I remember her!" Benny said quickly.

Jessie shook her head. "Of course you do. When there's food involved, you never forget, do you?"

"Never!" Benny said proudly.

"I've heard that a lot of adults like Mr. Finch's books, too," Henry said. "That must be why she was reading this."

Jessie sighed. "So I guess this isn't much of a clue after all."

"No, I guess not," Henry told her. "But we should return it to Mrs. Blake."

"Okay, we'll stop by her house later." She slipped the book into the back pocket of her jeans. "Let's go to the next car."

They opened the door to the fourth car, which was also the last. Unlike the other cars, this one was very dark because the shades were drawn. And there was an unusual odor in the air.

"What's that smell?" Violet said. "It's like some kind of medicine . . . "

Jessie sniffed. "Hmm . . . you know something? It's kind of familiar."

"It is?" Violet replied.

"Uh-huh. It's . . . " She sniffed again. "Oh, I can't remember! But I'm sure I've smelled it before."

Henry said, "I was thinking the same thing, Jessie. Let's search the car and see if we can find out where the smell is coming from."

Violet slid a few of the shades back to let in more light. As she did, the children noticed something else unusual.

"Hey, there's no trash in here," Benny said. "It looks as if someone already cleaned this car."

"Could Pete have done it?" Violet wondered. "Maybe he was in here before."

"We'll ask when we're done." Jessie said.

Henry saw something lying in the first seat. He reached over and grabbed it.

"If someone did clean out this car already, they missed this." He held up a shiny silver wrapper. "It's from a granola bar." He slipped it into his trash bag.

The Aldens went through the rest of the seats one by one, but the remainder of the car was just as Benny had suggested— spotlessly clean. They did notice, however, that the peculiar odor they smelled earlier became a little bit stronger as they moved towards the back.

"I don't see anything else in here," Jessie said, "We should go."

They stepped back outside and found Pete again. He had moved to another train and was giving it a good wash. The children set down their trash bags. Each was about half full and neatly knotted.

"Thanks so much," said Pete. "Did you find any clues?"

Jessie took the book from her pocket and held it up. "We found one of Mr. Finch's books. But it looks as though it belongs to one of our neighbors. Her name is written inside."

"That doesn't sound like much of a clue," Pete commented.

"No," Henry said, "that's what we thought. And there wasn't even any litter in the fourth car."

"That's because it was closed during the trip," Pete told him.

"Closed?" Jessie asked.

"There weren't enough passengers. Sometimes the conductors will do that—if they don't have enough passengers to fill all the cars, they'll close some of them. It's easier for them. It also makes it easier for me because I have fewer cars to clean afterwards!"

"Is there any reason there'd be an odd smell in the fourth car?" Henry asked. Then he described the strange odor.

Pete thought for a moment before shaking his head. "Nope. But I'll have to check it out if it's that bad."

Henry looked at the others, then said, "Okay, well, thanks very much for your help, Pete."

"And for letting us search the train," Jessie added.

"No problem," Pete said, shaking all their hands again. "If I can do anything else, just let me know."

As they began walking back to the library, Jessie said, "Based on what we found, it doesn't seem as though Mr. Finch was on the train."

"But we *know* he was on it." Violet pointed out. "Remember he called the library to say he was getting on the train?"

"So where'd he go?" Benny wondered.

No one had an answer.

CHAPTER 4

A Quiet Place to Read

"This is just terrible," Ms. Connally said when the Aldens gave her the bad news. "I've never had this happen before. An author no-show! I hope he's okay."

"We'll find out what happened to him," Jessie said confidently.

"If you can't, I'll have to call Mr. Van Buren," Ms. Connally said.

"He's the man who was here before, right?" Violet asked.

Ms. Connally nodded. "Right. He was the one yelling by the front desk before he stomped out. He doesn't seem to like Gilbert Finch or his books."

Henry said, "You should've seen what he did to that display of Mr. Finch's books we put together yesterday." He told her the story.

"Why would he do something like that?" Benny asked.

Ms. Connally shrugged. "I have no idea, Benny."

"I've never heard of any of Mr. Van Buren's books," Violet said.

"They're very good, actually," Ms. Connally said. "But they're for older children. Henry, you might like them."

"Maybe he had something to do with Mr. Finch's disappearance," Jessie said.

"We should keep him in mind," Violet said.

Jessie checked her watch again. "Okay, let's finish eating and get back to this mystery."

"Right," Henry said. "We don't have much time."

"Thanks very much for looking into this, kids," Ms. Connally told them. "I appreciate your efforts, but if Mr. Finch doesn't show up by, say, tomorrow morning, I'm going to have to plan for Mr. Van Buren to be here instead."

* * * *

"A lot of people will be disappointed if Mr. Finch doesn't make it," Jessie said as they walked along one of Greenfield's sunny sidewalks. There were big, beautiful homes on either side of the street. "And I don't think Mr. Van Buren will draw as big of a crowd. He's such a grouch."

The Aldens stopped at the house of Mrs. Blake, the woman who left behind the copy of *The Secret of the Pyramids* they had found on the train. There was a swing on the porch that could hold two people, and a sign by the front door that read, "All Friends Welcome."

The Aldens rang the bell and waited. The door swung back to reveal an elderly woman in a floral dress. The Aldens smiled, and Mrs. Blake smiled back.

"Well, it's so nice of you to visit me on this lovely day. Is your grandfather with you?" Mrs. Blake said.

"No, ma'am," Jessie said. "Not today."

"Probably snoozing in his easy chair," she said with a playful look in her eye, "when he should be in the backyard cutting the lawn or something."

The children laughed. They always loved the way Mrs. Blake joked about their grandfather.

Jessie took Finch's book out of her back pocket. "Mrs. Blake, I think you left this on the train this morning."

Her face changed from happy to surprised. "Yes, I did! I was wondering where it went!" She opened the screen door and motioned for them to come inside. As they stepped in, Jessie handed her the book. "I was reading it during my trip, and then I thought I put it in my bag. I didn't realize I'd lost it until I got home." She looked at it fondly. "Oh, thank you so much."

"You really like his stories?" Benny asked.

"I sure do!" she replied. "Hey, if you kids

can enjoy them, I can too! And I can't wait to meet him at the library tomorrow night!"

"Well . . . there might be a problem with that," Jessie told her reluctantly. "It seems as though Mr. Finch has disappeared."

Mrs. Blake looked stunned. "Disappeared?"

"That's right." Henry told her what they knew so far—that Mr. Finch definitely got on the train in Clairmont but wasn't there when it arrived in Greenfield.

"Oh my goodness!" Mrs. Blake said.

"That's why we came over," Jessie told her. "To return your book, and to ask if you saw him."

"No, I didn't," Mrs. Blake said right away. "I would've recognized him."

"That's what we figured," Violet said with a long sigh.

"Did you notice anything unusual?" Henry asked. "Anything that might be a clue?"

She thought for a moment. "No, I don't think so . . . Let's see. I got on at Briarwood. I decided to read his book on the trip, to pass the time. I bought it at a little store up there. I remember getting on the train and trying to read it, but it was too noisy. There was a dog barking somewhere. Can you believe that? A dog on the train? So anyway, I went to the very back, where it was quiet."

"The third car," Jessie said.

"Right, the third car. And then I started reading—" She stopped, and her eyes widened. "I managed to read in peace for a little while. And then . . . you know what? I *do* remember something unusual."

"Really? What was that?" said Violet.

"We went into a very bad thunderstorm . . . "

"Yes," Jessie said. The children remembered the conductors' wet uniforms.

"We stopped at one of the stations," Mrs. Blake continued, "and I heard someone yell '*Hey!*' behind me. I was surprised because it sounded like it was coming from the very last car, and no one was supposed to be in that one."

"Because it was closed," Violet said.

"Right," Mrs. Blake told her. "They didn't have enough people to fill it. Anyway, I heard this person yell, and I got up to see who it was. I looked through the window and I saw someone jump off just as the train was pulling away!"

"Wow, just like that police detective did in *Diamonds in the Dungeon*," Benny said.

"That's right," Mrs. Blake said. "I was thinking the same thing when I saw it."

"Which station stop was it, Mrs. Blake?" Henry asked. "What town?"

"I'm not sure," she said. "It was one or two stops before Greenfield."

"What did this person look like?" Jessie asked. "Did you get a good look at them?"

"No, it was raining too hard. But whoever it was, he or she was definitely in that fourth car."

"So there *was* someone back there!" Benny said.

"It looks that way," Henry said.

But if it was Finch, why would he jump off a moving train in the middle of a thunderstorm?

CHAPTER 5

A Very Strange Message

The children met their grand-
father at the Greenfield Diner for dinner. The
place was bustling with customers. The air was
filled with the hum of conversation, the clink-
ing of silverware, and the wonderful scent
of many different meals.

Sitting in their favorite booth, the Alden
children gave their grandfather the details
of this latest mystery. Meanwhile, they only
picked at their dinners. Grandfather soon
gave up hope that his grandchildren would
show much interest in food while they were

working on this case. Benny didn't even order dessert!

"Too bad we don't have Mr. Finch's cell phone number," Henry said. "I'm sure he carries it with him wherever he goes."

"We'll have to tell Ms. Connally what's happening," Jessie said. "We should stop over there before we go home tonight to give her an update."

"And then what?" Violet asked.

No one had an answer to that. They all fell silent.

Benny had been listening quietly, munching on his chicken strips and sipping his milk. But then something caught his attention from the other side of the room.

"Hey," he said in a whisper, "look over there!"

He pointed to a man sitting in a small booth by himself, drinking coffee.

"What?" Henry asked. "That man?"

"No, the bag!"

There was a brown leather bag on the other seat. It was very handsome and looked expensive.

"What about it?"

"Look at the initials, near the top!"

Sure enough, embroidered right into the leather just under the zipper, were the initials 'GXF.' All at once, the Aldens remembered Mr. Finch's full name: *Gilbert Xavier Finch!*

"Oh my goodness!" Violet gasped. "Do you really think . . . ?"

"How many other people have those initials?" Jessie said. "A middle name that begins with *X?*"

The children studied the man carefully. He was dressed in a navy blue T-shirt with long sleeves, plus blue jeans and a pair of well-worn work boots. He had dark hair with flecks of silver, and he looked as though he hadn't shaved in a few days.

As he took another sip from his coffee, the waitress came over and asked if he wanted anything else. He shook his head and took his wallet from his pocket. The waitress left the bill on the table, and the man set a five-dollar bill on top of it. Then he got up, taking the bag with him.

"Well, if we want to find out, we'd better move fast," Henry said.

The children filed out of the booth, followed by their grandfather.

Outside, the man paused for a moment to put on a pair of glasses.

"Excuse me, sir?" called Jessie.

The man turned suddenly, surprised to see the Aldens. "Yes?"

"I know this is going to sound like a strange question," Henry said, smiling, "but may I ask if that's your bag?"

Now the man smiled back. "No, it isn't. Er . . . how did you know that?"

"We think it may belong to a friend of ours," Violet said. "Did you find it on a train, by any chance?"

The man looked even more surprised, and also a little bit impressed. "Yes, as a matter of fact I did."

"On train number sixteen?" Jessie added.

Now the man laughed. "Yes, that's exactly right. It just so happens that I'm the engineer!"

The children looked at each other. Now

they were getting somewhere!

"And was the bag . . . on the fourth car?" Benny asked him. "The one that was supposed to be closed?"

The man nodded. "Indeed it was, young man."

"So Gilbert Finch was there," Violet said. "He must've been the person who jumped off!"

Henry explained the rest of the story. "And we thought Mr. Finch might've been in that fourth car."

"I guess he was," the engineer commented. He slid the bag off his shoulder and handed it over to Henry. "I found this in the overhead luggage rack of the fourth car. When I do find something valuable and I can't find the owner, I then have to report it. That means I have to fill out all these boring forms and stuff." He rolled his eyes. "Not much fun at all. So if you can return the bag to Mr. Finch, that would be great."

"We sure will," Jessie said. "Thanks."

* * * *

Back at the library, the children told Ms. Connally everything they knew so far. Then they set Mr. Finch's bag on a table in one of the back rooms and unzipped it.

"I feel weird going through it," Violet said. "I'm sure it has some of Mr. Finch's personal things in here."

"But there might also be something that helps us find him," Jessie pointed out.

On the top layer, the children found several copies of his books, mostly his new one. Underneath that, a cell phone charger, some clothes, and a leather bag with a toothbrush, shampoo, and other toiletries inside. And under that was a small notepad.

Jessie opened the notepad and began reading.

"Anything important?" Henry added. "Any clues?"

"Hmm—*Food shopping on Thursday . . . Do laundry on Friday . . . Booksigning up in Clearwater on the fifth of June . . . Fix that broken window on the second floor . . .*" Jessie sighed. "Not very interesting."

"That's it?" Violet asked.

"There's one more page," She said, flipping to it. *"Might need new dining room table . . . Have someone mow the back lawn . . . What should I do about . . . "*

"What is it?" Henry said.

"Okay, *this* might be a clue—it says, *What should I do about Van Buren?"*

"So we're back to him again," Violet said.

"You know what?" Henry said. "We should go through the library's catalog to see if we can find any information on Mr. Van Buren and Mr. Finch. You know—newspaper or magazine articles, maybe something on the Internet. We need to know more about this strange connection."

"Good idea," Jessie agreed. "Maybe we can figure out why Mr. Van Buren's name keeps coming up."

The children began to look through the library for any information they could find. After about an hour, they had gathered a small stack of newspapers and magazines. They each took a few and began going through them.

"According to this article," Violet said,

"Mr. Finch loves animals. It says he has given lots of time and money to various animal charities, and that he has kept dozens of pets through the years. It also says he refuses to eat any kind of meat. Only fruits, vegetables, and—listen to this—granola bars!"

Jessie nodded. "It *had* to be him in the fourth car of the train."

"In this magazine," Henry told them, "it says he sometimes likes to write in what he calls a 'secret country hideaway'. But he refused to tell the writer of the article where it was. He would only say that '. . . *it used to be a big old barn, painted red. It has since been re-painted white with black shutters and now looks quite lovely. I go there every now and then because it's so quiet and peaceful out there in the country.'*"

"What about his relationship with Mr. Van Buren?" Violet asked. "Anything about that?"

"Yes," Jessie said, "I think I found something. In this article, Mr. Finch said, *'I'm thrilled my books are doing so well. As long as they do better than Daniel Van Buren's, I'll be happy.'"*

"In this interview," Henry added, picking up a printout of an Internet article he'd found, "Mr. Van Buren said, *'I'm glad my readers enjoy what I write so much. As long as they stay away from that silly stuff Gilbert Finch comes up with, they'll be okay.'"*

"In this one," Violet went on, "Mr. Finch says, *'There are two types of books a youngster can read—good ones, and those that are like Daniel Van Buren's.'"*

Benny said, "Wow, they don't like each other very much, do they."

"Apparently not," Jessie said. Then she noticed it was nearly eight o'clock. "We'd better get going," she told them. "Grandfather is expecting us."

* * * *

When the children got home, they found a surprise waiting for them.

"I came in and saw the light blinking," Grandfather explained as he stood by the answering machine in the kitchen. "At first I thought it was a message from all of you. I quickly realized I was wrong. Listen—"

He hit the PLAY button, and out came one of the strangest messages the Alden family had ever heard. There was so much noise Henry turned the volume all the way up and still only a few words could be understood.

"Let you know . . . had no choice but to . . . he jumped off . . . lost in Allerton . . . terrible storm . . . going to Mr. Bean's . . . soon as possible . . . "

And there the message ended.

"It's Mr. Finch!" Benny shouted.

Jessie looked closely at the little screen on the answering machine.

"The call came in at 10:32—over six hours ago!" she said.

"And we've been out all day," said Henry, "No wonder we didn't know about it."

"Oh my goodness, I hope he's all right!" Violet said.

"Why don't we try calling his cell phone now?" Henry suggested.

"I thought we didn't have the number,"

Jessie pointed out.

Henry nodded. "It should be there on the answering machine, on the caller ID."

Jessie looked down and saw it. "Oh yeah. Good thinking!"

She tapped in the number and waited. Everyone else watched her, holding their breath.

After a few moments, Henry said, "Is he answering?"

Jessie shook her head. "No, it goes right to his voice mail."

"It doesn't even ring?" Violet asked.

"No." Jessie let out a long sigh. "Looks like this mystery is getting thicker rather than thinner."

"He said he was going to a 'Mr. Bean's,' didn't he?" Jessie asked.

"That's what I heard," Violet answered. "But who's Mr. Bean?"

No one knew.

"And what town did he say he was in?" Henry wondered. "Allerton? That must've been where he jumped off. I've never heard of it."

"It's about fifty miles up north," Grandfather said. "It's a nice little place. I've driven through it a few times. Very quiet."

Violet's face lit up. "Oh my goodness! Allerton! I've seen that name before!"

"You did? Where?"

She paused for just a moment to think about it one more time and make sure she was right. Then she looked at the others.

"I saw it in one of the articles we found at the library," she said. "It's where Daniel Van Buren lives!"

CHAPTER 6

A Smell to Remember

The children were up bright and early the next morning, talking in the kitchen. Jessie rummaged through the cabinets in the hopes of finding something they could eat, while the other three sat around the table.

"Maybe we should talk to Mr. Van Buren," Violet said. "Ms. Connally probably knows how to reach him. He might know something."

"Or maybe Mr. Finch is going to catch another train to Greenfield today," Henry suggested. "For all we know, he could just show up just like that—," Henry snapped his fingers, "—and the mystery would be solved."

"I think that 'Mr. Bean' person he mentioned in his message might be able to help us," Jessie said, pulling out a box of cereal. She gave the box a shake and mumbled, "There's not enough in here for everyone." She sighed and looked at the others. "Until Mrs. MacGregor comes back, we'll have to wait to eat." Mrs. MacGregor, the housekeeper, had left about an hour earlier to do the weekly grocery shopping.

"Or we could go down to the bakery and get some fresh bagels," Violet suggested.

Benny's face lit up. "That's a great idea! I love bagels!"

"I think you love everything at the bakery," Henry said.

Benny rubbed his stomach. "I really do!"

The Aldens filed out of the kitchen and down the hallway towards the front door. Watch, their always cheerful dog, ran up to see what was happening.

"Bye, Watch!" Benny said, rubbing behind

the dog's furry ears. "We'll be back shortly. Be good!"

Violet stroked his head. "I'll throw the ball around the backyard for you later, okay?" Watch seemed to understand and wagged his tail wildly.

Jessie knelt down for a lick on the face. He put his front paws on her knees and reached up to give her one.

"Ooo, you're such a good dog." She leaned in close to give him a quick kiss on the head.

Then she froze.

"Oh my goodness!"

"What is it, Jess?" Henry asked. "What's wrong?"

Jessie turned to them, her eyes wide. "I remember that smell now! The one that was in the fourth car!"

"You do?" Benny asked.

"Yes—it's *dog shampoo!*" She looked up at her older brother. "Henry, remember? That awful stuff we used on Watch a few weeks ago, after we found a few fleas on him?"

"Hey, that's right!" Henry knelt down and sniffed Watch, too. "Yes, this is definitely the same smell."

Violet and Benny were puzzled. "What dog shampoo? What bath?" Violet wondered. "Benny and I don't remember that."

"You and Benny were with Grandfather that day," Jessie said. "At the fair."

"Oh yeah," Violet said. "We were having our faces painted."

"And we had ice cream!" Benny said. "I remember that!"

"We decided to give Watch a bath while you guys were gone," Jessie continued. "We went to the pet store and asked for a good shampoo for fleas and ticks. They gave us this stuff that worked really well, but it had a strong medicine smell." Jessie sniffed Watch again. "It's still on him, even after all this time. Ugh—awful!"

"And that's the same smell that was on the train?" Violet asked. She was stroking her chin and thinking. "Could that mean that a dog was in the fourth car with Mr. Finch?"

Jessie's eyes widened. "Possibly! Maybe it was that dog who was barking! Remember Mrs. Blake said she heard a dog barking, and that's why she couldn't read?"

"That's right," Henry continued. "And that family we saw at the station, with the two children who were crying. Didn't one of the children have—"

"A *leash!*" Benny said.

"Yes, a leash," Henry told them. "But they didn't have a dog with them. I'll bet that's why the children were so sad. Something must've happened to it."

"Like what?" Violet asked.

"I have no idea," Henry said. "But maybe someone down at the station does. Let's go check it out."

✳ ✳ ✳ ✳

When they got to the station, though, they didn't see the conductor. But there were other faces they'd seen before.

"Look!" said Henry. "Wasn't that family on the train yesterday?"

"Yes," Violet said. "I remember the two crying children."

"They're not crying now," Benny

noticed. "But they still look sad."

The two children were helping their father put up flyers around the station. They carefully stuck bits of tape to the corners of each flyer so that their father could hang them up. Their mother stood nearby, dabbing at her eyes with a tissue.

"Should we talk to them?" Jessie wondered.

"Let's read one of these flyers, first," said Henry. They found one posted near the front door. LOST DOG, it said in block letters across the top, above a photo of a small dog with woolly fur.

"Poor thing," Violet whispered.

Below the photo was written: *Just as we arrived home to Greenfield on the Saturday morning train, we discovered our dear dog, Max, missing from his carrier. We don't know what happened and we are heartbroken! If anyone has any information that can help us find Max please contact the Taylor family.* A phone number was listed at the bottom of the page.

"We have information," Henry said. They all nodded. They walked over to where the family was busy putting up another flyer.

"Excuse us," Jessie said softly. "You're the Taylors, right?"

They all turned. "Why, yes," said the mother.

"I'm Henry Alden, and these are my sisters and my brother," said Henry. "We're trying to solve a mystery of our own, and we think your dog might be part of it."

The Taylors all looked at each other, and back to the Aldens. "Go on," said Mr. Taylor.

Henry told them the whole story. At the end, Mr. Taylor took the copy of the Finch book that Henry brought along and studied the photo on the back. "You know something, this man does looks familiar." He held it up so his wife could see. "Isn't he the person who patted Max on the head as we were waiting for the train to arrive yesterday morning?"

Mrs. Taylor only needed to take a quick look at Mr. Finch's picture. "Yes, that's him. He was very friendly," she told the Aldens. "And he seemed to have an instant connection with Max. Max doesn't always like strangers, as we said before, but he liked Mr. Finch right away."

"Oh, is that his name?" Jessie asked.

"Yes, Max," Mrs. Taylor replied.

"We're not surprised that he liked Mr. Finch," Violet said. "Mr. Finch loves animals. Max must've sensed that."

"Do you know how he got off the train?" Henry asked.

"We have no idea," Mr. Taylor said. "That's why we're putting these signs up. We're hoping maybe someone on the train saw what happened."

"He wasn't with you during the trip?" Benny asked.

"No," Mr. Taylor replied. "He was in the last car, in a cage, by himself."

"The fourth car!" Violet said.

"That's right," Mr. Taylor went on. "And when we went back to get him when we arrived here in Greenfield, he wasn't there."

"We looked everywhere," Mrs. Taylor added.

"He must've gotten loose and jumped off somewhere," Mr. Taylor finished, shaking his head sadly.

"Why was Max in the last car?" Henry asked.

"He gets nervous around strangers and tends to bark a lot," Mrs. Taylor replied. "So we thought it best to leave him back there, alone."

"We were really worried when we went through the thunderstorm, though," the father added. "Max is very afraid of loud noises."

"I went back to check on him during the storm," Mrs. Taylor said, "and he seemed fine."

"Did you see anyone in the fourth car when you went in?" Jessie asked.

"Oh no, I didn't go in. I just looked through the window. If I'd gone in there, he would've gone crazy as soon as he saw me. He would've wanted me to take him out of there."

Henry asked, "What does he look like?"

"He's very small," Mr. Taylor told them. "A miniature schnauzer. He's mostly white, with a little black nose and a few black marks. And he's got plenty of hair. It's short but kind of thick, almost woolly."

"If he did jump off, where do you think he would go?" Jessie asked.

"He'd be scared," Mrs. Taylor said, "because he wouldn't know where he was. He would hide someplace, like under a tree or a bush."

Jessie nodded. "We'll keep that in mind. Thank you for your time."

The Taylor's little son stepped forward. "Are you going to find Max for us?" he asked.

Jessie knelt down in front of him. "We're going to try our best. Okay?"

He managed a tiny smile—probably his first smile since he learned that Max was missing.

"Okay," he replied.

✳ ✳ ✳ ✳

The Aldens finally made it to the bakery, where they sat around a small table in a quiet corner and ate their bagels.

"All right," Jessie said, "so now we know there was a dog on the train, and that he somehow got loose and jumped off."

"And we know that Mr. Finch was in the

fourth car with the dog because he left his briefcase there," Violet added. "We also know he ate a granola bar, dropped the wrapper, and jumped off the train."

"Do you think Mr. Finch could have taken the dog with him?" Benny wondered.

The others shook their heads. "No, why would he do that?" Violet asked. "He'd never steal a dog."

Then Henry said, "Wait a minute! What about this—what if Max got loose, became scared, and jumped off the train, and Mr. Finch *went after him?*"

Jessie nodded. "That makes sense. If the dog suddenly jumped off and Mr. Finch saw it, I doubt he'd just stand there and do nothing."

"But where?" Violet asked. "Where did they get off the train?"

"Mr. Finch already gave us that piece of the puzzle," Jessie told her. "In his phone message."

"Allerton!" Benny said.

Jessie nodded, proud of her little brother. "That's right, Allerton."

"That name again," Henry said. "You know what? I think it's time we went there."

"I agree," said Jessie."

"And you know what else?" Henry continued. "I think we're going to get lucky, too . . . " He reached into his back pocket and pulled out the train schedule. "The next train heading north out of Greenfield leaves in less than an hour."

The Aldens finished their bagels quickly and hurried out.

CHAPTER 7

An Old Friend

The Aldens' minivan pulled up to the train station. "Are you sure you kids don't want a ride to Allerton?" said Grandfather.

"That's okay, Grandfather," said Jessie. "We're looking for clues around the train station. Why not take the train?" The other three children nodded.

"And it's fun!" Benny chimed in.

"Indeed it is," said Grandfather. He knew his grandchildren well. "Call me if you need anything," he said as the children climbed out of the van.

"Thank you," they replied together.

By the time the children had bought their tickets, the train was waiting at the station.

"Here we go," said Jessie, as they climbed aboard.

* * * *

When the Aldens got off the train at Allerton, they noticed signs of the thunderstorm from the day before. Wet leaves and branches were lying everywhere, and huge puddles had formed in the parking lot.

"Wow," Violet said. "That must've been quite a storm!"

"So, if Max jumped off the train, where would he go?" Henry wondered. He took a good look around. Then he spotted the parking lot. "How about over there?"

Jessie said, "If I was a small dog caught in a thunderstorm and scared, I'd look for the first place where I could get away from it, just like the Taylors said he would. Under a car would be easy enough."

"Let's check it out," Henry said.

They searched from car to car, and after awhile it didn't look as though they would find any clues. They figured Max would have gone to a car close to the tracks. But there didn't appear to be any sign of this.

Then Violet looked under an old red truck that was parked near the back of the lot.

"Hey!" she called out, "I think I found a clue!"

As the others hurried over, Violet stood up with something in her hand—another granola-bar wrapper.

"That's the same kind as the one we found in the fourth car yesterday!" Jessie said.

"Except this one is all chewed up," Violet pointed out, holding it up so they could see the little dent marks all over it. "Also, it still has some granola bar inside. Yuck!"

Henry said, "You know what? I'll bet Mr. Finch used it to lure Max from under this truck. He was probably too scared to move otherwise."

The others nodded. "That would explain

the way this is all torn up," Violet said. Then she tossed it into a nearby garbage can.

"But it doesn't explain where they are now," Jessie added. "What do you think?"

"Don't forget, Mr. Finch said something in his message about going to see someone named Mr. Bean," said Benny.

Henry smiled. "That's right, Benny—good job." He pointed to a phone booth across the street. "There's a phone book in there. Let's see if anyone in Allerton has the last name *Bean.*"

The children looked through the phone book and found two people with the last name *Bean.* The Aldens decided they would call them both.

Violet picked up the phone. "There's no dial tone," she said.

"The phones must still be out from the storm," said Jessie. "Let's see if any of the shops down the street have a phone that is working."

Then, suddenly, Violet started to giggle.

"What, Violet?" Jessie asked. "What's so funny?"

Violet said, "Maybe the people in that shop will be able to help us."

"Really? Which one?" asked Henry.

She pointed down the street.

"That one," she said.

And there, standing on the corner, was a store with a big sign that read, "Mr. Bean's Coffee Shop."

* * * *

All four children were still giggling when they went inside. It was a charming little place, filled with the aroma of coffee and delicious baked goods like warm corn muffins and soft chocolate-chip cookies.

The Aldens found four empty stools at the counter and sat down. A young waitress with blond hair spotted them and came over.

"Hi, kids, what can I get for you?" The nameplate on her uniform read, 'Jenna.'

They each ordered milk and a small desert. Henry had a bear claw. Jessie asked for a cherry turnover. Violet got a black-

and-white cookie. And Benny, hungry as ever, ordered two cookies.

After Jenna set their plates down, she asked, "Would you like anything else right now?"

"Well, we have kind of a strange question to ask," Jessie began.

"Oh? What's that?"

"Yesterday, some time in the afternoon, did a man come in here with a little dog?"

Jenna laughed. "Sure did. It was that Gilbert Finch character!"

The Aldens were stunned. "You know him?" Jessie asked.

"Of course. We all do. Hey George!"

The door to the kitchen opened, and a man wearing a white apron came out.

"Yes?"

"These kids are asking about Gilbert, when he came in yesterday with that dog."

George gave a little laugh, too. "Oh, it's always interesting when Gil comes in here," George said. "We gave him a towel so he could dry off the dog, who was so scared he was shaking. Then Gil got him a little bowl of milk. They both sat in here until the storm died down."

"Did he try to call anyone?" Violet asked.

"Couldn't," George said. "The phones haven't been working since the storm. One of the main lines must've been knocked out."

Then George pointed to a large photograph in a frame that was hanging on the wall.

"See? He's been coming in here for ages."

It was another picture of Mr. Finch. At the bottom he'd written, *To George and Jenna, who make the best coffee in the whole Northeast. Your friend, Gilbert Finch.* Right next to it, the Aldens couldn't help but notice, was the signed photograph of another famous local author—Daniel Van Buren.

And the inscription he wrote was, *I agree with everything Gil said.*

CHAPTER 8

The Little Engines That Couldn't

"I think you were right, Henry," Jessie said, still staring at the two pictures. "Mr. Finch and Mr. Van Buren don't seem to be enemies at all."

"And I was thinking about something," Violet added. "Remember that book Mr. Finch published a long time ago called *Lost in the Mountains?*"

"That was one of the best ever!" Benny proclaimed.

"It sure was," Violet agreed. "And remember the dedication page? He wrote,

'This one is for Danny Boy.' What if Danny Boy was Mr. Van Buren? His first name is Daniel, after all."

"And there was also a character in that story named 'Dennis Van Bowlen,' wasn't there?" Jessie asked.

"That's right," Henry replied. "I'll bet Mr. Finch named him in honor of Van Buren. The two names are certainly very similar."

Jessie was nodding. "I think it's clear where we need to go next."

"It sure is," Henry replied.

✳ ✳ ✳ ✳

Jenna was kind enough to give the Aldens a lift to Daniel Van Buren's home during her lunch break. As soon as they made their way down the winding gravel driveway the house came into view, they all stopped, speechless.

"Are you all thinking what I'm thinking?" Jessie asked.

"I think so," Violet replied.

Daniel Van Buren's home was clearly an old barn. It was painted white, but a few cracks around the edges revealed that the original color was red. And the shutters on either side of the windows were black.

"Just like in that article we read," Henry said.

Violet was nodding. "*This* is where Mr. Finch sometimes goes to write. This is his secret hideaway!"

"So much for them being enemies!" Benny said.

Standing on the front step, they rang the bell and waited. A moment later, the enormous door flew back, and an older woman stood there with her hands on her hips.

"Yes?"

"Uh, I'm sorry," Jessie began, "but could you please tell us if Mr. Van Buren is home?"

"No, not since early yesterday. Who may I ask is calling?"

"We're the Aldens," Henry told her, "and we're trying to find a friend of his. His name is Gilbert Finch."

"Ah yes, Gilbert. He was here up until a little while ago, I believe. I'm Rita, Mr. Van Buren's housekeeper."

"Oh, okay," Henry said. "Well, we need to find Mr. Finch. You said he was here?"

"Yes, although I'm not sure when. I've been visiting my sister since yesterday afternoon, so I've been out. But Gilbert has his own key, and he sure left a mess for me to clean up."

"What kind of a mess?" Violet asked.

"Wet clothes?" Jessie guessed.

"Muddy shoes?" Henry added.

"Yes, that's right. How did you know?"

"We're detectives!" Benny told Rita, and then Henry gave her a quick rundown of everything that had happened so far.

When he was finished, Rita said, "Well, maybe you can tell me what this is, then." She turned the broom around and pulled out some fine white hair. "I've never seen anything like it in the house before."

Jessie took a handful and examined it. The others did the same. There was little doubt as to what it was . . .

"*Dog* hair," Jessie said.

"Dog hair?" Rita groaned and shook her head. "I'll have to do the floors again."

Henry said, "Do you mind if we come in and take a quick look around for more clues? If we see any more dog hair, we promise to clean it up."

"Sure. Just don't make a mess."

"We won't," Jessie assured her.

They went from room to room, looking and not touching. There was a small laundry area in the back, with a washer and dryer. The children found two small bowls on the floor. One still had some cracker crumbs in the bottom, and the other had a tiny puddle of water. Then they found Finch's rain-soaked clothes in the sink—a handsome houndstooth blazer, a torn white dress shirt, and a pair of black leather shoes that were probably very nice at one time but now appeared completely ruined. And lying in a nearby trash can was a cell phone. When the Aldens tried turning it on, nothing happened—it was ruined.

When they went upstairs, they found two

towels piled in a corner of Van Buren's guest room—one was stained with dirt, the other had more fine white hair all over it. It also had that same horrible dog-shampoo smell that was in the fourth car of the train.

"He must've taken a shower with one towel, and dried off the dog with the other," Henry said. They also noticed that the bed had been slept in. It was still unmade.

Jessie picked up the telephone on the nightstand and put it to her ear. "Still doesn't work," she said. "So that explains why he didn't call us again."

The others nodded as these pieces of this mystery fell neatly into place.

"But then we end up with the same problem as before," Jessie told them. "Which is . . ."

"Where is he now?" asked Violet.

"We keep missing him!" Benny said.

"Exactly," Henry replied. "We're on the right trail, but we're too far behind."

Violet looked at a pendulum clock that was hanging on the wall. "And there's so little time left before the reading at the library!"

Then Jessie said, "I've been thinking . . . if you came here out of the blue, just like Mr. Finch did, stayed the night, took some clothes and some food, and then left—and the person who owned the house was an old friend—wouldn't you leave a note of some kind?"

"I certainly would," Violet said.

Henry snapped his fingers. "Hey, remember in that one book of his, *The Jade Flower of Japan*, when the boy left the message for his mom by putting it on the computer?"

"Oh yeah!" Jessie said. "Then he turned off the screen so those guys chasing him wouldn't see it!"

"But he knew his mom would, as soon as she turned it on again."

"Do you think Mr. Finch did that here?" Violet asked.

"It's worth checking out," Henry replied. "We didn't see a note anywhere else, and Van Buren is probably on his computer every day. It's the perfect place to put it."

The Aldens hurried down the hall and back into Mr. Van Buren's office. It was a warm and cheerful place, especially for anyone who liked to read—the walls were covered floor-to-ceiling with bookcases and filled with books of every kind. Three huge windows provided a breathtaking view of the hills and mountains beyond. And in the center of the room was Van Buren's enormous oak desk, covered with papers and more books. His computer was running, the children could tell, because they could hear the hum of the hard drive and the whir of the fan. But the monitor—just as in Finch's story—was off.

"Here goes," Henry said, pushing the button. It took a moment for the screen to light up, but when it did, they knew they'd been right. The message was right in front of them. Henry read it aloud:

Danny Boy,

Sorry about the mess—so much has happened since yesterday. I'll give you the details when I see you. In the meantime, I have to go to the library in Greenfield to meet with some readers. Since I missed the train and there aren't

any others scheduled to go down there today, I'm taking your other car, the old one. I hope you don't mind!

–Gil

PS—I read some of your new book—the one that's sitting on your desk here—and it stinks.

Henry chuckled. "Just what I thought—they don't hate each other. They're just rivals, that's all."

"What's a rival?" Benny asked.

"Someone who's trying to outdo you. Mr. Van Buren is trying to sell more books than Mr. Finch. But they're obviously good friends. They just enjoy teasing each other. That's all Mr. Van Buren was doing at the library when he was moving around Finch's books—just giving him a hard time. They've probably been doing it to each other for years."

"And what about this other car?" Jessie said. "Does Mr. Van Buren have an old car?"

Then a voice came from behind them,

and it certainly wasn't Rita's voice.

"Yes I do," Daniel Van Buren replied, standing in the doorway. "And it appears that my friend Finch has taken it. But it has a little problem, I'm afraid—it doesn't run very well."

CHAPTER 9

The Road Less Traveled

At first the children thought Mr. Van Buren was going to be angry because they were looking for clues in his house. But as he came into the room, a smile spread across his face.

"Rita, my housekeeper, told me what you kids were doing, so I figured I'd drop in and say hello."

He came over and shook their hands, then leaned down to read the message again.

"Stinks, huh?" he mumbled to himself.

"Boy, he's got some nerve . . . " Then he looked back at the Aldens and folded his arms.

"So, we've lost our friend, have we?"

The children were still too stunned by Mr. Van Buren's tall, imposing figure to say much. Finally Henry said, "Yes, sir. You see—"

"Sir?" he said with a laugh. "Don't call me that, young man. It makes me sound old! 'Daniel' will do fine."

Henry looked at the others and shrugged. "Well, okay—Daniel." Henry told Mr. Van Buren everything that had happened up to this point. Mr. Van Buren listened patiently, nodding and stroking his chin.

When Henry was finished, he said, "First of all, I have to tell you all that I'm very, very impressed with your detective skills. I'm guessing you kids do this a lot."

Jessie chuckled. "You have no idea."

"Well, your experience shows."

"Except that we still don't know where Mr. Finch is," Violet pointed out. "And we're running out of time!"

Mr. Van Buren smiled. "Ah, you'd rather have Gil at your library than me, huh?"

The children were quick to say no, of course not, but Mr. Van Buren knew better.

"That's okay, his books have always been a bit more popular than mine, the little rat. But that'll change someday," he said.

"For now, though," Jessie said, "We should go find him."

"And get Max back to his family!" Benny added.

Mr. Van Buren nodded. "That's right," he said. "Okay, everyone, I'll do the driving. To the garage!"

* * * *

The main road between Allerton and Greenfield was a three-lane highway bustling with cars and trucks moving at high speeds. Van Buren drove a big car that groaned like an old lawn mower. The children, strapped into their seats, looked everywhere for signs of Mr. Finch as they bounced along.

"I was building that other car in my free time," Van Buren told them, speaking loudly because of all the road noise. "It's sort of my hobby, fixing up old cars. Then I sell them and give the money to charity."

"That's so nice!" Violet said.

Van Buren nodded. "I get to do something I enjoy, and people who really need money, get it. That way, everybody wins."

"If Mr. Finch took the car in the first place," Jessie said, "then it must run okay, right?"

"Well," Van Buren replied, "I don't want to bore you with technical details, but no. It'll run for awhile, but then it'll get too hot and conk out. He certainly won't be able to make it to Greenfield. He's got to be on the road somewhere, broken down."

Jessie checked her watch again. It was nearly four o'clock. They only had a few hours left.

One hour was wasted zooming up and down the highway, looking for any signs of Van Buren's car. The children called Ms. Connally to find out if perhaps Finch had somehow made it and was already there. He hadn't.

By five-thirty, the Aldens began to lose hope.

"He's not anywhere on this road," Violet said. "We've been up and down twice already. There's no way we could have missed him!"

Henry was still looking out the window, saying nothing. Then he suddenly turned around, his eyes wide. "Wait a minute!"

"Do you see him?" Benny asked.

"No, but I was just thinking . . . Mr. Finch probably left a few hours ago. The housekeeper said he wasn't there when she got back."

"So?" Jessie asked. She didn't see where Henry was going with any of this. Neither did anyone else.

"So, why would Mr. Finch take this road? He wouldn't need to hurry. He would've had plenty of time!"

A smile broke out on Jessie's face. "Oh yeah . . . "

"And that got me thinking about something else in his books," Henry went on. "Have you ever noticed how his characters always avoid main roads when they can?

How they always take back roads instead?"

Mr. Van Buren nodded. "Ah yes, that's right. And that reminds me of something else, too—I remember the first time Gil went down your way. He was visiting some old college friends who lived close to Greenfield. He decided to drive down instead of taking the train. The day after, he called and told me about this beautiful back road he'd discovered. He said it was so much prettier than the highway. All rolling hills and trees, which he likes. Quiet and beautiful."

"That has to be where he is now!" Benny said. "Let's go!"

CHAPTER 10

Some Explaining to Do

The back road was exactly as Mr. Van Buren had described it—quiet and beautiful. It cut through a valley surrounded by tree-covered hills. And a lazy river followed it most of the way, the sun sparkling on its rippled surface.

For the first half hour they saw no other cars at all. Jessie checked her watch one last time. "Six o'clock. Only an hour left. And it'll take us almost that long just to get back to the library!"

Henry nodded slowly. "Yeah," he said

with a sigh. "It looks like he's not here. And we shouldn't be late."

Mr. Van Buren added, "Oh well—I guess everyone in Greenfield is going to have to settle for me tonight!"

He pulled off to the side and began turning around. He decided to head back to the highway, where he could get to Greenfield faster.

Then Benny spotted something out the back window.

"Hey, wait a minute!" he said. "What's that over there? It looks like smoke!"

They all looked. Sure enough, far in the distance, there was a faint puff of smoke rising from behind the next hill.

Jessie said, "We should definitely check it out, but we have to hurry!"

Van Buren spun the wheel and sped off. As they neared the top of the hill, everyone strained to see over it. The moment they reached the peak, they saw the old green car, sitting on the shoulder with its hood up and smoke billowing from the radiator.

The Aldens let out a group cheer. Then

they had one last scare—when Van Buren pulled up alongside the old car, there was no one in it.

"Oh no!" Violet said. "He's not here!"

"Yes he is," Jessie replied, pointing through the windshield. "Right there!"

They saw a man a few hundred feet ahead, going down the lonely road on foot, with a little white dog next to him. Since Mr. Finch didn't have a leash, he had attached his necktie to Max's collar.

Gilbert Finch was walking to Greenfield.

✳ ✳ ✳ ✳

Van Buren pulled up alongside him and said, "Hey, stranger, need a lift?"

Finch looked more tired than anyone the Aldens had ever seen. He was filthy and sweaty.

He still managed a smile, though.

"Danny boy! Fancy meeting you out here! Here in . . . uh . . . "

"The middle of nowhere?" Van Buren asked.

"Yeah, pretty much."

Then Finch noticed the Aldens. He pointed to them and looked back to Van Buren. "Nieces and nephews?" he asked.

Van Buren laughed. "No, but I believe you already know them—they're the Aldens, from Greenfield."

"The Aldens!" Mr. Finch said, clearly shocked. He stepped forward and stuck his head in the window. "What are you doing all the way out here? Shouldn't you be back at the library, waiting for me to not show up?"

The children were almost out of breath from laughter.

"Hop in and they can tell you the whole story on the way," said Mr. Van Buren.

"Okay," Finch said. He opened the door and let Max jump in. The dog scurried to the back and jumped right into Benny's lap. Finch shut the door and put on his seatbelt.

"If we hurry, we should make it just in time for our talk," Van Buren said.

"Sounds good," Finch replied, then said, "Wait a minute. *Our* talk? What does that mean?"

"Uh, we'll have to explain that, too," Mr. Van Buren replied, smiling.

Mr. Finch looked back at the Aldens helplessly. They just shrugged.

As they got moving, Henry whispered, "This should be a very interesting trip."

* * * *

The two authors argued all the way down to Greenfield—whose books were better and why, whose books would still be famous in a hundred years, whose books had spelling mistakes, and so on. But through it all, the Aldens could tell that Finch and Van Buren were old friends.

Just as they reached town, Henry said, "Mr. Finch? Can I ask you something?"

Finch turned around, leaning an arm over the back of the seat. "Sure, Henry."

"It's about Max," he said, nodding towards the dog. Max hadn't moved from Benny's lap the entire trip. "How did he get loose in the first place?"

"Ah, well, that was my fault I'm afraid.

When the train passed through the rain-storm, Max began whimpering. I couldn't just sit there and do nothing, so I unlocked his cage, took him out, and sat him on my lap. I tried to quiet him down by stroking his fur and talking softly to him, but it didn't seem to help. So I put him back in the cage, and I guess I didn't lock it right, because a few moments later he was jumping off the train!"

"But how did he get out of the car in the first place?" Violet asked. "Surely he wasn't strong enough to open that heavy metal door!"

"No, but I was," Finch told them. "You see, one of my favorite smells in the world is the air on a rainy day. After I put Max back in his cage, I opened the door when we stopped in Allerton to take a deep breath. The rain was coming down really hard, and it smelled wonderful. So I was standing there with the door open and my eyes closed, and the train started pulling out of the station. That's when Max scurried past me and jumped out the door!"

"Ah," said Henry, "and you felt you had to go after him—"

"Right, because I'm the one who let him out in the first place."

"Okay," Henry said, nodding. "That makes sense."

"That also explains why you left your bag on the train," Jessie said. "You didn't have time to get it."

"I wasn't even thinking about it," Finch told her. "By the time I realized I'd left it on the train, I'd already caught our little friend over there." Then he asked, "And how did you know I was in the fourth car on the train? No one was supposed to be there."

"The granola-bar wrapper," Jessie said. "We found one there, then another one in the parking lot, and in your briefcase."

"You used one to try to get Max out from under that red truck, right?" Violet asked.

"That's correct."

"And what about that note in your notepad?" Violet went on. "The one about Mr. Van Buren? You wrote, 'What should I do about Van Buren?'"

Finch laughed and looked at Van Buren. "Just a reminder to myself. I was trying to figure out whether or not I should stop in and visit him on the way back from Greenfield."

"No need to worry about that now," Van Buren said.

"Nope."

"And your cell phone? It stopped working?"

"Right, it got all wet. I managed to make that one call to your house before it died. I had no charger, either, and none of the phones in Allerton worked." He laughed and shook his head. "Can you believe it? With all the technology we have today, I couldn't get a message through just a few towns away."

They pulled into the library parking lot and were shocked to find the entire crowd standing outside on the lawn, waiting. Jessie had called Ms. Connally during the trip to let her know what was happening. Ms. Connally was thrilled that they would have not one but two great authors appearing that evening. Grandfather was there, too, looking very proud. So was Mrs. Blake, holding copies of all her Finch books, ready for him to sign.

The Taylors had made it as well. The moment Finch opened the door of Van Buren's car, Max jumped out and raced over to them. The two children were so happy to see their dog again! Max jumped on them and licked their faces, his tail whirling around like a propeller.

As everyone got out of the car, the crowd began clapping and cheering. Finch and Van Buren waved and smiled. The Aldens stepped aside, but then Ms. Connally told them the crowd was applauding for them, too.

"If it wasn't for the four of you, this wonderful night would never have happened!" she said.

The children grinned. When the applause finally died down, everyone began walking inside.

Mr. Finch turned to Mr. Van Buren and

said, "You know what, Danny Boy?"

"What's that?"

"I suddenly have a fantastic idea for a story. It's about these four smart youngsters who have to find a crazy old man who foolishly got lost on his way to see them."

He turned around and smiled at the Aldens, who were too startled to say anything.

"Sounds like a winner to me," Van Buren said, patting his old friend on the shoulder. "I wonder what our faithful readers will think?"

"I'm pretty sure *I'll* like it!" Benny said, grinning.

THE END

GERTRUDE CHANDLER WARNER discovered when she was teaching that many readers who like an exciting story could find no books that were both easy and fun to read. She decided to try to meet this need, and her first book, *The Boxcar Children*, quickly proved she had succeeded.

Miss Warner drew on her own experiences to write the mystery. As a child she spent hours watching trains go by on the tracks opposite her family home. She often dreamed about what it would be like to set up housekeeping in a caboose or freight car—the situation the Alden children find themselves in.

While the mystery element is central to each of Miss Warner's books, she never thought of them as strictly juvenile mysteries. She liked to stress the Aldens' independence and resourcefulness and their solid New England devotion to using up and making do. The Aldens go about most of their adventures with as little adult supervision as possible—something else that delights young readers.

Miss Warner lived in Putnam, Connecticut, until her death in 1979. During her lifetime, she received hundreds of letters from girls and boys telling her how much they liked her books.